RESURRECTION

A COLLECTION OF WORK BY
JOHN J. McNULTY, JR.

Riverhaven Books

RESURRECTION is a work of the author's creation, published posthumously. The stories were likely inspired by his experiences and prompts in the courses he attended at Boston University.

Copyright © 2021 by Virginia Young

Published in the United States by Riverhaven Books,
www.RiverhavenBooks.com

ISBN: 978-1-951854-19-5

Printed in the United States of America
Edited and designed by
Stephanie Lynn Blackman
Whitman, MA

Dedicated to those

who left their imprint on a world

they left too soon

TABLE OF CONTENTS

PREFACE

The eldest of six, John J. McNulty, Jr. was the son of Mary (Sieller), a nurse, and John J. McNulty, a Hartford, Connecticut police officer.

Upon completion of high school at age eighteen, John Jr. enlisted in the Navy. Two weeks later his younger brother Francis lied about his age and enlisted in the Marines.

The family photo below was taken while both boys were home after basic training. Our parents must have been grateful to have their family together again even briefly. In the photo I am sitting on John's lap – I was two. Also pictured are my sisters –Lorraine, with dark hair, Therese, a blonde, Fran in his Marine uniform, and David who was seven years my senior.

The two eldest boys went off to war, and through letters, remained close. John was assigned to a PT boat in the Pacific and Fran ended up on Iwo Jima.

Weeks passed, war raging around each of these young men, neither knowing if the other was still alive. The PT boat John was on received orders to pick up Marines on Iwo Jima. John reached out his hand multiple times, rapidly pulling men on deck. Then he found his hand entwined with that of his brother.

After twenty-five years on the Hartford police force, my father was offered a position in Boston, Massachusetts. We moved to Weymouth and shortly after, both boys came home safe.

At the age of twenty-one, John entered Boston University to study for a career in writing. He thought to be a journalist and a fiction writer on the side. His collection of manuscripts, commented upon and graded by his professors, are positive with all A's. He was thought to be an exemplary writer with a maturity beyond his years.

On October 26th, 1947, John Jr. died in an automobile accident. Our family was forever changed. We all suffered the loss. Although I had a brief measure of time with my brother, I remember him well. He was the family favorite to every one of us. He told me when I was being too fussy, and he taught me to love classical music. He bought me the album *Peter and the Wolf*, which I still have, and he made me listen to it as he explained what was happening. Then I had to listen and tell him the story in return. He danced around the house with me to the Strauss Waltzes and Ravel's Bolero. He nick-named me Jinx – why I am not sure. Perhaps he thought as I did that Virginia was too old a name for a little girl. Even now, I miss him terribly. At the completion of his life, he was twenty-three, I was six.

For seventy-three years John's writing has been resting in a black leather valise, waiting. It's waited far too long. I tried not to change anything, leaving his voice to be heard. Reading from his elegant handwriting style in black ink, there were times I had to guess the word as I transferred the stories to my computer, all the while thinking what magic he could have performed if he'd had such a device at his disposal. I am a painter and writer of fiction – fifteen novels, and not one of them could compare to John's work. At the time of his death he was talking to television executives about converting one of his pieces to a play. Everyone was saddened and shocked with his loss.

My hope is that you will read every word in this collection. Look at his handsome face on the cover and wonder what propelled that young man to write of maturity, heartbreaks, failings and fears, and – above all else – love. His stories capture concepts that society, even today, struggles with. It reminds us that these ideas are not new – the notion of being true to one's self, of taking chances, of living for what is good and right. I believe if he had lived longer, he would have written so much more, imparting greater ideas into our world, leaving it a better place.

Thank you, from John.

~Virginia Young

AMONG THE SHADOWS

The wind blew cold. Revolving ventiducts atop the apartment houses grated a harsh metallic squeal into the night chill and beyond, into the cobalt, stark sky.

He tasted the air, winter was good. He trembled from the chill but liked it. He was comfortable, aware of himself. He thought about cats, how they coiled into themselves, warm, unconcerned, and selfless, detached and satisfied. He wasn't sure he liked cats, but he did like the severe and demanding wind.

Cats had a femininity he wasn't sure he trusted. They had grace, and he liked that. But then, it was all retroactive, women were a lot like cats. Most of them made themselves comfortable, warm, cuddling close. And they purred, too, accompanying neck-nibbling kisses, biting one's lips, or lightly caressing one's throat while reaching into the unbuttoned shirt and bare skin. Yes, women were cats, who liked to be touched, but hesitant for that concentrated connection, gentle to defined or brutal. He laughed as the correlated scenes played over and over in his mind. He closed his eyes for a moment then laughed again feeling the vacuity within.

And then he thought of Michele. Strange that he'd thought of her as little, frail. No, Mike wasn't frail. She was strong, strong with independence. She was poised, femininely lithe, and gentle yet singularly unlike other women.

He thought of how he unconsciously paralleled her strength of character with the unexpected brawn of her arms and core, and of her thighs as they'd pressed to his when they danced, or when they'd sat behind the shrubbery in the park so they could speak without the interference from others. That defiant need for privacy had surprised him.

And her voice was soothing to him as well as vibrantly exciting in its clarity and the deep mauve shadow of its tone. She had the ability to give purpose to common words and power to what her mind composed, coloring her thoughts with bold conviction – a sense of being unafraid. He determined that they were alike in more ways than they differed. He enjoyed recalling the sensation of his strong arms around her small, unresisting body. She was something.

He walked along in the cold and smiled inwardly, knowing that they shared an insatiable clash and mutuality. And he knew that he loved her completely. Physically and emotionally, they were a match as much as they were often contrasted.

Fear enveloped him. Afraid of loneliness, he felt a chilled space between them. Disquietingly they'd touched fingertips at first, in a mockery of fullness. He'd struggled to understand their relationship and failed. The love he'd felt for her was complete, the warm lips against his caused trembling and uncertainty, as though he wondered if she feared relinquishing more than she'd intended. Now he was left to remember that within the last week she'd seemed withdrawn. He tried to remember, his mind hungry for answers. Had one simple word caused this division of hearts? Should he have kept the word *love*, slipped half silently, to himself?

He thought of the night sitting on the bench, his coat draped over her legs, his arm around her shoulders. In his speaking he had quivered with deep emotion those penetrating words, *I love you.* "You are my nucleus," he'd said. "I want all I ever am directed to you. That is my dream."

The words spoken, she'd turned to him for a kiss then softly said, "I like that dream."

They'd walked the dark, cold streets, the somber brownstone buildings shining faint rays of light from the occasional window. One after the other there were deep-shadowed doorways where three or four granite steps led students and professors to peace and privacy, and then there was Blakely House, a women's dormitory: tall, straight-edged,

2

and sterile. They had stood together, he not wanting to leave. His lips brushed hers and then she turned away. He lightly kissed her eyes and when he felt her move backwards just inches, he moved his hands to his jacket pockets. She stood in a shadow, her expression hidden. He wasn't sure he was breathing as he turned, said a soft-spoken goodnight, and left. He turned once to see her moving toward the dormitory door as if in slow motion. What had he done? Convinced he'd said too much, he felt an immense sadness.

Arriving at his building, he entered the alcove and placed his hand on the brass latch of the heavy door, opening it to a dimly lit hallway. He turned toward the street before closing the glass framed in thick wood and noticed the barren sky, no stars, and the branches of leafless trees seeming to mock their nakedness. Streetlights struggled with the dark, and a red neon sign stood on a first-floor windowsill. On another sill close to the door he saw what was left of a geranium, left to the cold, dried and rustling in the soft night wind – careless death.

It was two days later when they stood in the dormitory hallway, quiet with the weekend population of students home or off to what they could afford to do for fun, a walk in the park, a movie, dinner with friends. Michele kept a foot's length between them, staring at her feet and then at his eyes. It was painfully awkward. She turned away, looking at nothing.

"Mike," he began, half choking the words, "look at me." He lifted her chin, her eyes meeting his again. "I love you. I'm sorry if that frightens you. You're everything to me; you're my religion, Mike. I'm here to assure you that we can take things as slow as you wish. Marry me, Mike; we could be wonderful together."

She was trembling as she gripped his arms and pressed her face to the folds of his coat, concealing her expression.

He felt the pulse pounding through her body and recognized the tension of a frantic animal when it was planning escape. A vacancy reared high in his thoughts, an emptiness which had been conceived days before. She looked up at him and brushed tears aside. "I knew you were going to ask, Louis. I was afraid you would. It was all inevitable. I just knew you were going to ask," she said, once again chasing the tears away. "How could you expect me to know, Louis? I don't know. I don't know. You should have left it as it was. We could go on that way, just being together. That's all. No other way. Louis, Louis."

She pressed her slim frame to him and cried, standing there wrapped in one another's youthful emotions. He felt the tremors of her body while his own felt numb. He could find no words.

He barely said "see you later" as he walked out of the building, feeling empty to the point where he wondered if he could actually take a step never mind walk several blocks back to his own small apartment. He loved her and he'd unintentionally failed her with rushing the deep urge to clarify his feelings. He was ready for love, she was not. What had he done?

Allowing time to mend broken spirits, Louis waited several days to meet with Mike again. He wasn't sure what he'd say, but he wasn't going to mention commitment, marriage.

He entered Blakely House and waited silently. The matron came from the lounge, a tall woman, thin and erect, her face finely pleated and expressionless.

"I'm calling on Miss Zaroff," he said.

The matron's eyes narrowed as her expression turned to contempt. Louis staggered inwardly at her reaction without knowing why. "Miss Zaroff has left here," the woman said, her tone emotionless.

Louis closed his eyes for a moment then stared at the woman as she spoke. "There's a note for a Mr. Burton. Are you…"

"Yes," Louis said. "I'm Burton." He felt flat inside. He could have wept. He took the note and left. Beneath a streetlight he tore it open and read. "I can't love you, Louis. Mike."

He read it again, six short words, that was it. He walked along the street with the note in his hand, unaware that he was moving, breathing.

Days passed with Louis's pencil tracing aimless lines on blank sheets of paper. He threw the pencil aside only to take it up again and to throw it further. Thought after thought he felt weakened. He looked up and saw himself in a mirror. He thought of love, how it didn't always line up with another, and of distant voices advising him to get through it, this deep loss.

***

Without a knock on his door, with no sound he was aware of, the door opened and Mike stood there, her coat thrown open, feet slightly apart, hands at her sides. "Don't move, Louis. Don't. Don't say anything. I've come to speak. Don't stop me. I might not say what I need to.

"I know these last days must have been hell for you, the same way they were hell for me. No, stay there, Louis, please stay there in that chair. I'm here because I love you. I love you more than I care about what you're going to think of me. I know you're hurt and I hate that it's because of me. I never meant to be the darkness in your life.

"Please, Louis, don't get up, please let me finish. You don't completely know me and that was my intention. My own fears of rejection kept me silent, distanced. But at Blakely they know. I became careless." Leaving her coat draped across a chair, her hands trembled at the buttons of her dress. With an unsteady voice, her complexion pale and pained, her eyes closed to tears, then she looked up to his face.

"They threw me out, Louis, when they found out what I am. This is what I am, Louis. Look." With the last button unfastened, the dress fell to her ankles. Louis felt his throat close, his heart trembled. He closed his eyes, oblivious to anything around him. When he opened his eyes a few moments later, she was gone – she who was a he; not Michele, but Mike.

***

Louis didn't know how many hours or even days he'd sat there, a pencil moving dumbly over a sheet of paper, tracing the mute ache of his soul, tracing the annihilating loneliness which shrouded his being. He sat, a man without a world, herded into the dark corner of unmitigated aloneness, shackled to his own flesh and his uncompromising and convulsing isolation. He wrote without knowing why.

I hear young laughter in the streets at night, young effervescent feminine laughter mingled with frolicking male voices. I conjecture about worlds beyond mine, of joyful worlds. A pall of nameless depression descends over me. Will I ever know such youthful spirit and vital love? It seems leagues away, unattainable. What sort of fool am I?

Beauties of the world expend themselves futilely – and lips which should open before mine are pressed to cold rock lichen. I perceive nothing but endless torture of remoteness; the materialization of my world is a malcontent thing, ever insatiate, ever groping beyond itself, ever void of common blessings.

> *The pen is cold and lifeless, dull,*
> *And gropes for words to tell.*
> *What may one say?*
> *Beneath the hull,*
> *Sea's changing moods on having swell*
> *Are told, and nature's ways are lucid clear;*
> *Unlike the cluttered mind which blunders on,*
> *Strives, falters, lists in fen of fear*
> *That shadows seen mark dreams forgone.*

He cast the pencil aside, the sheets of paper fluttering to the floor – he sat huddled within himself and thought. He thought of his love for Mike on one side, and Mike standing, feet slightly apart, a pale young body against a dark blue dress – a man's body revealed.

What was love, this emotion which rose and coiled in the path of human life, which grew out of sexual desire and created loneliness and need and shattered independence? What was this thing humans

6

worshipped? Or did they worship themselves instead? Yes, maybe that was it. Love is a selfish thing, or how else would something so altruistic, so devoted at the same time, be so demanding? Selfishness, that was the strength of love. And what was sex, the insatiate need for it?

He thought of the great dream, of the strong clash and mutuality of being, of that which had destroyed the child and made him half of what he'd expected to be. Love was the great compliment. "I love you, Mike. I love you more than I want anything else – you are my reason for existing." He remembered the words from Mike, "I love you, Louis. I love you more than I care about what you're going to think of me."

The words were pale yet fierce in the night. Words knowing no boundary, torn things seeking birth in human flesh and mind, agonized utterances. And there was Mike seeking the right, knowing the right, afraid of it. Love without boundary. Michele. Michele the woman in love, Mike the man wracked, alone. "I love you, Louis."

I love you, Mike. I love you, Mike. He buttoned his coat against the night chill and walked. *I love you, Mike; you are my religion.*

KIDNEY AMONGST THE DUNES

New York and nostalgia are synonyms in my mind. Webster would promptly order my execution on the dreariest of dawns were he aware of such thoughts – I have never lived in New York. In fact, I have never been there for longer than one week at a time. To take this further, I don't suppose that, placed end upon end, my Manhattan sojourns would constitute around six months. But no matter, I am strangely content to call it home, sublimely content in trying resilience of the word *hours* by application of chosen vagrancy and leer of affection. Call it my passion for a cottonwood in Queens if you wish.

Anyway, I had an unorthodox time in New York (the traffic-light system never ceases to amaze me with its efficiency) four years ago. There words should stop, but no. I was in the town of two-dollar cocktails and decided (rashly) to call an acquaintance of mine. I called him.

He was (it's past-tense, notice) a munificent fellow and commenced showing me the town, though I had previously been in most of the curio corners of the metropolis. Eventually we arrived at the Museum of Art. I should have foreseen such, but then if I had I'd not have troubled to call him. However I coughed into the folds of my topcoat and determined to make the best of what promised to be a tedious time. And it was as I'd guessed when that mausoleum of classicism had in view. We entered and passed like a Battery-bound subway (I was trailing him) through all of the exhibits, pausing only momentarily (I know not why) for a period of venerable silence before Mona Lisa, then on again until we reached the exhibits of the postimpressionists and surrealists. You see, this particular friend of mine is a zealous disciple, though not an artist, of the *new school,* and an indefatigable champion of said intellectual depths.

Had I not been aware at the time where I was, I'd have immediately conjectured that the chamber of the cubists was a strange place for

Gold Seal Linoleum wares. Unfortunately, such was not the case, for one could have dismissed that lightly enough. I was subjected to at least forty-five minutes of around-the-room walking, bewildered, gazing; and suffered also the gestures and delineations upon the soul expressing there. I'm afraid I was so unenthusiastic as to be chided for my missing vision, imagination, and sensitivity. I admitted my density and listened in awe and incredulity with respectful silence. I was just a lump.

I recall in particular one of the most modern of linear addicts, one Piet Mondrian. I believe he is so vivid in my mind since I happened to come upon a photograph of him one time in which he posed without allowing his body a single curved line, quite an incredible feat. He looked like a human ashtray composed of verticals and horizontals. I remember, too, the admiration which was in my friend for that man. And I recall a work of his, *Study in Red.* It had approximately five lines arranged at right angles, attached to one another in the most soul-searing manner possible, and in one small rectangle was a dot of red as though there quite by accident. *Study in Red*, ah yes. In all due respect to those devotees of Mondrian, I'd be willing to wager that there is a tile design in a lavatory in an apartment house on Mountford Street in Hartford, Connecticut which is making off with the Mondrian talent.

And so we exhausted the works of the postimpressionists and left the geniuses of straight lines and half faces to the echo of the museum, and I offered as an antidote the cryptic recesses of the Kretchina, The Grotto on 46th Street, or even Jack Dempsey's. But that was met with a chill stare of injured intellectuality. I knew my terror was not over. I was humbled. I followed meekly to the Virginia O'Brien, Salvatore Dali Dungeon. They didn't like Dali a great deal. He's an exhibitionist and not a true portrayer of the subconscious, I was told, but his withered, melted watches are full aesthetic concept (I continually thought of them with a side dish of gravy.) And I was told, too, that the beauty of Miss O'Brien's *Pelvis in Distance* was the extent of imagination, the exploring mind of the woman, examples of the deeply thoughtful intellect. I was then firmly convinced that I was the rudest of clods.

We proceeded from the debacle of modern art to the Hurricane Club, where using a menu and a napkin, I drew several lines, colored a square talentedly with my pencil, calling it *Study in Graphics*. My ability as a cubist was verbosely thrashed into obscurity.

It might be that I am insane. I have often wondered who was the judge. I admit that I know little of art, but I do know what I appreciate. I presume that I'm as out of character digressing upon paintings as the man who suddenly finds himself in the lingerie department in the labyrinth of a five-and-dime store while searching for a two-way electric socket. I must indeed be an audacious sort then. I am aware that concepts alter, but one does not expect the cataclysmic reactions so visible. I would suggest other releases were I not afraid of offending. The billboards are a lucrative industry I understand. But then, I suppose I am an insensitive swain.

Sic transit gloria mundi – Thus passes worldly glory

NO MORE DECEMBER
(1939 – 1947)

The hallway was dark. His feet clumsy, he stumbled up the creaking old wooden stairs. Lurching between balustrade and wall, he grumbled and pulled himself upward, the banister beneath his right hand feeling smooth and fragile.

He stopped for a moment as he mounted the last step. Breathing laboriously, he swayed giddily then rubbed the back of his hand across his face and heard the rasp of three days' beard. He moved toward the pale edge of light which marked the base of the entry – he swore softly as he kicked an empty kerosene can, then opened the door and stood there.

"What're you doin' back here?" she said, her voice hard.

His eyes were tired as he leaned against the door jam and looked across the room at her. She sat in the battered mohair chair, a copy of a movie magazine draped across her bare leg, a faded pink negligee carelessly open exposing her body. Cigarette butts littered the worn floor. She snapped a black garter on one putty-flesh thigh for effect. "Well?"

"I'm hungry," he said. "It's been three days. I need something to eat and a drink."

She motioned to a bottle. "Gin," she said. "Take that and get out, you alky bastard." Her voice grew high pitched. "And don't come around here askin' for food, you hear me? You have a job. I've had two men in three days – what've you been up to? I need to feed the baby, food's gone. You can't even pimp right."

"No food, nothing?"

"Not unless you want some of this," she gestured as she held one bare breast toward him then covered it loosely.

11

"Come on, Agnes," he said turning away.

She laughed in a brittle tone as he took a drink from the bottle of gin. He felt the warmth of the liquid mingling with his insides. He took three more gulps and felt his hands become steadier, the trembling barely visible. He tightened the bottle's cap and slipped the glass vessel into a jacket pocket.

"Get out!" she said. "More customers, not two in three days, ya hear me? Do your job! Maybe then I'll have somethin' to feed ya. You're soft and scared; I was a fool to marry you. What in hell was I thinkin'?"

He turned from her and walked to the door, to the stairs and the paneled door leading to busy streets of downtown. His eyes to the sidewalk, he felt the cold penetrate his lean body. It was snowing, and it was Christmas.

Red and green neon lights flickered spastically from above him – L-E-O-N'S – onto the slow-falling snow. Red and green reflected in gray-brown slush at his feet from compassionless drivers in fast cars. A blue English Bulldog's head glared dully through the opaqueness of the vapor-fogged plate-glass window next to a door he entered.

"Hey! Merry Christmas, Charlie!" A rotund white-haired man hurled the greeting with a smile.

"Yeah," Charlie murmured. "Merry Christmas."

"Here's to yuh," the man on the stool next to him said as he downed several swallows of a frothy beer.

Charlie nodded. "How's the kids, Paul?"

"Cold," Paul said before swallowing more beer. "Hey, it's Christmas. I'll buy you a beer. How're *your* kids doin'?"

"Cold," Charlie answered.

Glasses were drained, conversation was sparse. The bar was frigid from the front door opening and closing. Charlie glanced around the room and noticed bodies pressed close to the mahogany bar as if it emitted warmth. A small piece of holly stared through the tobacco smoke from a corner of a large, flecked mirror before him. Three eggs floated sluggishly in a jar of murky water. Charlie looked at the eggs and then to the faces around the bar. Everyone wore a somber face – no one in this place had whatever it was they wanted.

"Want a woman?" he dared to raise his voice so everyone could hear. "Fourteen Pine Street, Apartment three. Clean? Sure. Frenchy? Yeah, sure. Fourteen Pine, Apartment three. Rates are fair."

Charlie stood and walked out into the alley. He added a few gulps of gin to the contents of his stomach. He staggered out onto the sidewalk, avoiding the stench of the dark passageway. His thin-soled shoes slipped in the slush. He was tired. His legs ached with a dull pain, and he sat down on a length of granite near an iron fence to rest and take another swallow of gin. He sat still. He closed his eyes. The snow blew idly, gently against his face, large flakes like the tongues of cats against eyelids.

December again. He had married Agnes in December.

***

He switched off the headlights of his father's car. He turned to her – she did not move. He ran his right hand through her hair tenderly. She began to cry.

"Agnes, why, what's the matter, honey? What is it?"

She turned to him weeping against his jacket.

"What's the matter sweetheart?"

"Charlie, I don't know what to do. I'm afraid you'll be mad. An' I don't want you mad. Do you love me, Charlie? Say you do."

"Yes, sure, you know I do. Agnes, what's…?"

She covered her face for a moment then spoke. "Promise you won't be mad, Charlie."

"No, darling, what is it?"

"I'm goin' to have a baby, Charlie."

"What? Are you sure? Did you have a test, see a doctor?"

"I did. It's true."

Charlie looked from her tear-stained face to the traffic passing them by as they parked at the side of the in-town road. He looked at Agnes, her eyes fastened to his as though her life depended on his reply.

"Okay, okay," he said. "I need to think. We'll figure somethin' out."

"Charlie, you're gonna marry me, right? You said you loved me." He shook his head and closed his eyes before looking at Agnes. "Yeah, yeah, I'll marry you. We'd better do it soon, make it look legit." He leaned toward her, kissing her lips clumsily before starting the car.

***

"By the powers invested in me," the minister began, and it was then that Charlie looked down at his high school class ring on her hand. He hadn't even graduated yet.

***

Eight long years, years that should have been the best of their lives, but they weren't. He knew, as did Agnes, this was not a good match. The choices were few. He had no training, but Agnes did. Turned out their first baby looked nothing like Charlie and a lot like a football player on the high school team. By the time he figured it out, a second baby, his, was on the way.

Charlie leaned against the fence and the snow blew harder against his face and neck. He pulled his collar up, stood, and walked in long, swinging strides. He knew what he had to do. No longer drunk, he reached 14 Pine Street. He climbed the narrow stairway, opened the door, and entered.

She was sitting naked on the edge of the sink, a towel across one leg. "Hey, Charlie, this was a good night," she laughed. "Three guys in one night. Good pimping, Charlie boy, real good."

He walked over to her and watched – he'd never seen a woman do that. He watched for a moment then hit her. He hit her hard near the back of her left ear. She fell, the towel slipping from her leg. He turned her over, tied the towel around her neck, and pulled it tight.

***

"Is this your husband's body, Ma'am?" the police officer asked.

14

"Yeah," she said as she tied the belt on her robe.

I'll have to get more men – gotta give the pimp a funeral.

NOCTURNE I

The last time I saw Paris…a good song; memories come back. Is a guy nuts to remember? I don't know. I suppose it can be good, not sure, but I don't think so.

The last time I saw Paris…yeah, in the Bradford. Louise and the last time I saw brightness and laughter, and a wrinkled sort of sadness.

Give me another scotch, Mac. Yeah, same; like I said, yeah, thanks.

I loved her. "I love you, darling," I said. She loved me too, she said and smiled. She was quiet. She didn't say it again.

Make it another, Mac, forget the ginger.

Music played as a little French guy came out. His actions were clever, pretty good. Then he turned sad. He cried. He sang and cried and played a pantomime. Yeah, and I played too, I guess. The lips that laughed cried, and I wanted to shout that what was in him was in me too.

What was that guy's name? Pagliacci. Yeah. Sing you damn fool, sing Pagliacci! That was me and the last time I saw Paris. *La Marseillaise:* Louise singing and translating the French. That's the way it was. I loved her.

"I love you, Louise," I said.

She smiled and said nothing. She hummed sort of sad.

The scotch arrived and I took a nice swallow. Then the song, *Louise, 'every little breeze seems to whisper Louise.'* Yeah, perfect. "Your song, honey," I said.

"Yes," she said with a smile, and then, "Pull your chair closer to me. You're too far away."

"Check," I said, and to myself I repeated the words, *I love you, darling*. She smiled as I moved closer.

When the entertainer finished, we walked out. An elevator operator dropped us to the ground floor, his eyes to a dim light at the four-by-four's patterned ceiling. "Lobby an' groun' floor," he said. Louise said good evening to him as we left – I just nodded and smiled.

"Where to, kid?" I asked.

"Walk," she said.

I was glad. Nothing I like better than walking a long time with my arm around her. Louise was young, strong, I felt proud to be with her. *My god, darling, I love you,* I thought of her as we walked.

The cabs lurched by us and we hopped a subway out toward Cambridge. We left the tunnel and rattled along above the street. The lights of the hub spread out behind us and to the right, to the left and blinking out one by one were the lights of Beacon Hill. The elite ones you know. Then there was the river, wide, dark, with a few colored lights from boats. We headed along the edge and walked the esplanade – our long, slow steps in the night.

"It's beautiful," she said.

She had a way of speaking, you could feel her emotions.

"Great," I said. "The stars, look at them, and the water where it bends, like a part of the sky."

The night sky did something to me. I loved the smell of her dark hair and the way moonlight made it glisten. My face close to her, I could breathe in the fresh shampoo with perfume fragrance, kind of like gladiolas after the rain. I pressed into the smoothness of her neck. "I love you, kid," I said. Her hands said *I love you* back as she placed them at the back of my head.

"Let's walk," she said.

"Right," I agreed, but I didn't want to walk. I wanted to sit and think of how much I loved her; think of how lucky I was, how nice her black hair smelled, how it tickled my nose. I wanted to think of how sweet it would be sitting on a bench with her, my eyes closed, my head in her lap. Like sitting on a haystack in the evening, with dark coming in, and the pheasants playing in the leaves at the edge of the woods. It would be peaceful, the soft hay beneath you, the pheasants – just scratching those leaves – unaware of you. It's like being nothing. You can forget you're you. You think and have a smoke.

The coolness came in off the river as we walked. Little waves slapped against the rocks and shore and the wind blew through the bushes as I had my arm around her. My whole body ached with love for Louise.

We walked to the trolley entrance. I dug into my pockets for change as the train rattled and shook. It curved through the tunnel fast then stopped. It began to rain as we watched it together, the wind blowing it inside through a window where we sat. I tried to close it and couldn't. I wanted to give her my coat but she wouldn't take it. "You're sweet," she said, squeezing my hand as she moved closer.

"Sweet? Me?" I said. I wanted to laugh; I smiled instead. I wanted to say *I love you, Louise,* but I didn't.

Out onto the sidewalks again we watched the rain together, lights from cars bounced on the road like lightning and skipped off against the curbs. The water in the gutter carried some of the light away. Ever notice car headlights bouncing in the rain? Yeah, like they're dancing, floating and landing, windows catch it too, those little firefly bits of light.

The night air was cool as the leaves swayed leaving droplets falling all around us. We walked slowly, observing the rain lingering on wrought iron fences and granite steps. Streetlamp light found its way to the moisture, dressing iron and stone, and a large puddle fanned out at the corner. With my arm around her I said, "Jump, kid." We laughed then realized we were there.

The building where she lived looked dark in the mist, and the bricks were streaked where water had seeped through holes in the gutter and over the sides. We got there too soon. The night should have been starting. I wished it was just six o'clock and I'd be walking up to her door, feeling good. We'd go walking, and I'd be telling her what we could do, or ask what she'd like to do. All the while, thinking how much I loved Louise. But now it was over. I'd thought of a million things to say, and yet I said nothing. I didn't want the night to end.

We walked up the deep and rounded brownstone steps. It made me wonder, how many other guys had gone up those steps with their girls, feeling classy, wanting their evenings to last longer and thinking *I love you, honey.* I don't know, but we walked into the shadowy alcove. I could make out the white strips of paper marking the mailboxes and the bells for each apartment. Streaks of pale yellow from the streetlights ran down the gutter and large drops of rain fell from everything above us. It made a noise like someone snapping their fingers. Tires from a car going past the doorway slapped at the wet road. All evening, rain and occasional gusts of wind, but they didn't bother us.

Louise was quiet. She looked up at me. "I had a wonderful time tonight, Ben," she said, then placed her hand on my left arm.

"I'm glad," I said, feeling like a clown, foolish. And then the silence, it felt strange, awkward. I kissed her warm lips and pulled her close. She was soft against me, and I kissed her throat and then her hair. Again that sweet rain-on-gladiolas scent filled the air around us. "I love you, darling," I said.

"Don't, Ben," she said, and I felt the slight push of her hands against my arms.

What happened? Had I misunderstood her feelings for me? I felt drained, the passion gone, and why? Had I expressed too much? Had I frightened her, or had she never felt the same way about me? I tried to kiss her lightly again but she stopped me. "No, Ben," she said softly.

She looked away and I felt empty inside. She walked slowly to the door then turned to look at me, her eyes dim, clouded with sadness, the way they were when she hummed softly in the Bradford.

With her hand on the glass door leading to her second-floor apartment, she turned again and glanced at me before disappearing up the stairway, leaving me to feel numb.

I'm not sure how I navigated the steps from her building. All I could think of was the leaves on the trees dripping and the song, "The

Last Time I Saw Paris."

I made my way back toward my place, stopping for one more scotch. "And forget the ginger," I said.

THE LASHING SEA
(A fable in six parts, with prologue)

PROLOGUE

It was cool as they sat in the Green Hat sipping whiskey, shielded from brutal Manila sun. Heavy walls and shadow offered comfort, but there was the smell, inevitable of a ruptured city; of bomb-fractured, moist mortar; of blasted sewerage lines and earth-dispersed feces. And there was noise, intrusive clamor of long silenced horns, thin off-key violin and flat drums. The orchestra played and smiled; there had been a long silence.

Kirman raised his glass, a cut-down bottle. "Paths entwine," he said to Stuart. "God, it's good to see you."

"Prosit!" Stuart said. They drank and grimaced – Manila whiskey was poor. Kirman drew his right hand across his lips then returned his glass to the table.

"Four years," Kirman said.

"Yes, and the rendezvous in Manila," Stuart laughed as he placed his empty glass down. "Fair maiden Manila."

"Manila is presently an outhouse," Kirman said. "The Flips make good outhouses."

"The Flips make worse whiskey," Stuart said. "My Lord, who'd have thought a few years ago that we'd be swilling rotten liquor on the other side of a very big ocean?"

"I was young," Kirman said grinning. "An ocean was just a lousy lot of water to me, that's all. I didn't think. I was busy with a good time, no thought for changes." He laughed self-satirically. "Changes in life occurred only in women between the ages of thirty-seven and forty-seven."

Stuart reached for a book which lay face down beneath Kirman's arm. "Reading up on the love life polyps? Years Too Soon – or Late, by John Damon."

"I knew him," Kirman said. "I found the book in the Red Cross

21

lounge. He, by the way, was a man who knew that war was coming." Taking the book in his hands he thumbed through the pages then read: "Our times are marked by a great and defensively fearful nationalism. And within the definition of boundaries there exists individual economic chaos, vacillating and anarchic politics, and a resultant suspicious and aggrandizing diplomacy. The superficial preoccupations and insubstantial philosophies of our age will, unless there be an immediate metamorphosis, mature into another world conflict within the next twenty-five years.

"That was written in 1920 in Berne, Switzerland."

Stuart half smiled. "You knew this Damon?"

"Yes, I met him in '37. I was completing my last year at the University of San Francisco and doing a bit of writing myself. Damon was a weird man. He was possessed of a peculiar strength incredible of its facility. Are you interested in this?"

"Yes, go on," Stuart said.

"One wondered about his strength and never knew its source. Just as one wondered from where he came – I for one remained ignorant of that information." Kirman's voice softened. His words were clear and heavy. He spoke well as Stuart listened attentively to the story.

THE FABLE: PART ONE

Duonia Ramstlov rang the bell and waited. She counted the cars parked in the drive, twenty-eight, the usual Mitchell soiree. She felt sorry for her host: he'd surrounded himself with artists, writers, and composers, fostering them with cases of champagne and expensive liqueurs, and vicariously delighting himself with the towering delusion that he was one of them.

The door opened. "Good evening, Miss," the butler said with a polite nod as he stepped aside.

"Good evening, Carl." She handed him her wrap. "Where is Mr....Oh, there he is. Thank you, Carl."

Rod Mitchell walked toward her with a smile on his dignified face, looking much younger than his fifty-seven years despite his white hair. A well-preserved man, the evening clothes added to his striking appearance. "Duonia, so good to see you, my dear. Lord, you're looking lovely this evening, but then, you always look quite like a goddess." He took her hands in his momentarily and she laughed.

"Alright, Rod," she said smiling. "It's nice to be here."

He stepped near to her and turned so they could walk toward a large room together. "Come in and meet the others. And forgive me for being a poor host, but there are a few things I must attend to. Go right on in and introduce yourself to those you don't know and say hello to old acquaintances. Larson's in there, creating fabulous fictions as usual. He paints with more perception than you do, you know. He's really afraid of you. Well, excuse me, my dear, I won't be long."

"Of course," she said with a faint smile, her eyes scanning the sea of people.

She stood at the wide drawing room doorway for a moment, gazing over the group for a friendly face. She smiled at those who greeted her then walked to the cocktail table where George Kirman was swallowing some of his drink. "Hello, George. Strange to find you here."

Kirman grinned. "Don't be sarcastic, you lovely wench." He handed her a glass filled with champagne. She touched it to his and raised it to her lips. Aware that someone was staring at her, she did not swallow a drop. Glass midway to the table, her hand trembling, she knew instinctively who it was.

"He's here, Russe," Kirman said, smiling to mask his words

"Yes." A sluggish tension mounted within her. She turned and looked across the room to where he stood at the far end, a glass in his hand, one arm resting on a bust of Beethoven. He averted his eyes as their glances met. She continued to observe him, feeling a slight resentment; she was conscious now not only of him but of the fact that he reacted to her. The veil became more dense, more encircling.

She swore silently at herself, at her acute awareness of this man, at her inability to forget him. His strong face and dark piercing eyes had remained in her mind since Kirman had introduced them a week before. She had attempted to paint him – she had failed. In memory, she had been able to see only gentle nuances of the strangeness which shrouded him, gossamers with which she was not yet familiar and which seemed to reach out of him to embrace her. She had wanted to see him again; she had refused to admit it even to herself. Now she was aware of a feeling, vague fear, that tremulous desire to know the unknown, perhaps the unknowable. She turned back to her companion.

"He asked me if you were coming," Kirman said. "He seemed afraid to ask, kind of like a small boy."

She looked for some trace of sarcasm in his words, on his face; there was none. She thought she understood the shadow of which he spoke. She wished she possessed his analytical mind and was simultaneously glad she didn't. "Thanks, George."

She walked to a chair, knowing that the strong eyes of John Damon followed her. A limpness pervaded her, out of the urge to know this man, out of a fear that she would not, out of a counter and defensive urge *not* to know him, and out of a sweeping inclusive knowledge of her weakness before the inevitable. She wondered how long she could remain in the room with him. No one else seemed present; there were taut trembling wires between them conveying an undeniable intensity. Duonia wondered what John Damon felt; he appeared calm, detached. She regarded him closely, cognizant of only herself and Damon and the thin, silvery shadow of George Kirman. She sat, the fingers of her graceful hands tense.

She sipped her champagne slowly and watched Damon as he moved with the spasmodic steps of a paralytic among the groups of people. In spite of his gait, one did not see him as being maimed and pitiable, at odds with the physical infirmity of self. His walking seemed a part of his peculiar person, integral with being unbroken.

He turned his eyes to her. She stared back at him, a sensation of lightness in her breast. It was as though she looked into a great dark abyss and imagined a thousand variations of humanity. She hated that she trembled again. Her artistic eyes looked deep and saw dignity and humility, strength and an isolation which reached out of distance and gaunt loneliness to stand before her, indomitable, pained for warmth and proximity in its remoteness. Then the eyes hardened, fought back what she had seen, observed the secret anguish, and he glanced away, allowing her to catch only a partial glimpse of fear. She pondered: she had read humanism, and yet humanism out of a far removed world, frightening in its poignance, alien in its sensitivity, alone. She was aware of ephemeral echoes of herself posed against a broader backdrop. She could not understand; she *must* understand.

She arose from her chair and walked into the library, closing the door behind her, stopping the sound of numerous voices, protecting for herself the dimness and silence there. She sat alone on the floor before the hearth. She liked the warmth and light, and the flickering shadows it cast. She sat in the silence and heard only the occasional snap of a burning log. She knew why she had gone there, and she waited.

The door opened. She did not turn. She tried to prevent her hands from shaking. She could not. He walked into the room and stood near her. A chill passed over her body and she shuttered momentarily. She did not look up. They remained still for a time, each aware of the tension which rose between them, each afraid of the other, and each ignorant of the reason for the other's fear. Then gently he bent to offer his hands which she took, and he raised her, half carrying her to a chair. He was tender as he placed her there, steady as he gently pressed a strand of her golden hair into place. He stood near her, a strange expression about his eyes. She looked back at him. Then suddenly a trace of inexplicable fear passed over his face and he left the room hurriedly, his feet thudding against the floor in peculiar spastic fashion.

Duonia closed her eyes and let her head fall back against the chair. Fatigue pressed like a dark fog about her. She was tired.

She closed her eyes for a moment then stood and left the library. She sought out Kirman and lightly touched his arm. "Will you drive me home, George? I have a foul headache."

He scrutinized her closely for a moment. "Yes, certainly." He found her wrap and draped it over her shoulders before walking to his car. Before long they were out on the road. Kerman was driving swiftly through the night to San Francisco.

Duonia sat with her back pressed to the door, her eyes focused on the road ahead. Her hair flashed like sunlight in the glare of passing cars.

George stole glances at her, the finely molded features, the luxurious hair about her shoulders, uncurled and graceful. There was a strong frown showing deep concentration about her eyes; her hands were clenched tightly together.

"You don't have a headache," he said.

She closed her eyes for a moment then looked off to the side at darkness. "No."

"I know partially what you feel," he said.

"Damn you, George, for introducing him to me."

"He's a man," Kirman began, disregarding her words. "The most powerful and peculiar man I've ever known. You can't get him out of your mind, Russe; you won't be able to. It was the same with me. And then, you're a woman. He's a man we're drawn to. I'm not sure how anyone would not be drawn to him – he's brilliant, confident."

"He doesn't seem to be simply a man," she said softly.

"Yes, there's too much, too damned much. Or maybe *we* have too little."

There was silence for a short time before Kirman said, "There is a desert of anarchy. We have sown our own oases but the herbage of something larger draws us irresistibly, like a lodestone." There was a note of futility in his voice which spiraled about her – his voice described John Damon. She knew he was right.

THE FABLE: PART TWO

The day was clear with a strangely magical light, unearthly to Duonia, as if she'd been drugged. She knew as she descended the precipitous path that the day was as every other day – that this aura of fantasy emanated from within her, an irrational collection of thoughts. She stopped at intervals, leaning against the dark stone of the cliff, to combat the vertigo which overcame her.

The sea thudded heavily along the shore and crashed energetically against the great rock headlands at either end of the beach. Duonia was aware of the salted air, the cries of the gulls, with only a dream-like cognizance. Her mind was enmeshed in a vortex of writhing emotions in a weird unaccountable element of irrationality which never before had pervaded her thoughts. *Don't be surprised at whatever he is*, she recalled Kirman's words; words draped in shadow, words confirming what she knew without knowing. And she was afraid of the dynamic force, a fear which had grown out of the undeniable demands of the unavoidable.

She walked past the beach where she glanced at a portfolio which hung on the rail extending about the boathouse. She looked out beyond the edge of the landing and over the swells. He was not in the water. She crossed the sand toward a landfill which divided the beach and hid from her view the other end. As she climbed the rocks, her gaze swept over the cliffs which enclosed the small shoreline, which stood defiant, as if indestructible.

She came upon him unexpectedly. She stopped, startled, then pressed close to a massive boulder, quivering, caught in the whirling delirium of the utterly incredible man before her. She closed her eyes. She swayed, her hand to her forehead. He stood, back to her, only thirty feet away. His strong shoulders, tapering and powerful chest and flat muscular hips glistened with moisture in the sun – but his legs. She opened her eyes and looked again; the great, vigorous torso of a man, with the shaggy legs and cloven hoofs of a goat.

Half concealed behind broken rocks, unable to move, she watched him. He stood there, motionless, his body wet and gleaming in the penetrating rays of late afternoon. Then he ran as though driven by boundless, inexhaustible energy, his shoulders bent forward against the force of his speed. Duonia crouched still further from sight as he turned at the far extremity of the beach and came back. She did not move. She remained hidden there, mesmerized, as he raced back and forth at the edge of the water, running in rapid bursts and short strides and long springing leaps.

She watched him, entranced, for several minutes before she moved. Then she climbed over the boulders and waited with a sensation of weakness inside. He started back toward her, head down as he ran. Suddenly he sensed that she was there. He stopped abruptly, sand spraying away from him as he drove his hoofs deep. He regarded her for a fraction of a second then ran wildly to the cliff, madly leaping from ledge to ledge, his pointed hoofs finding holds in the almost sheer wall, sending stones and sheets of shale crashing to the ground below, until at last he could go no further. He stood on a ledge fifty feet above, bounding frantically against the smooth surface, springing like an imprisoned beast in effort to go still higher, yet failing and falling back to the narrow ridge which supported him. His leaps grew less vigorous and finally he stopped, his forehead resting against the cliff, his arms outstretched upward, his hands flat to the unyielding wall. He turned and looked down at her, his strong body shaking with fear, his eyes dilated in wild animal terror, his heavy chest rising and falling rapidly.

Duonia looked up at him, her hands at her sides as though in simple surrender, her body weak and strangely conscious of the wind which pressed her shirt and slacks tightly to her. She called to him, "John Damon, come down. It is I, Duonia. Come down. Come down."

28

The heaving of his chest subsided. His eyes lost the gleam of primordial madness and violent dread. He moved down the face of the cliff slowly, watching her as he did so. When he reached its base he called to her, "Turn around."

She turned and faced the sea.

He ran past her and dove into the breakers. Treading water he said, "Walk down to the landing." Then he moved swiftly, effortlessly through the swells.

When she reached the boathouse, he was clad in his beach robe waiting for her. They moved up the steep path together, his hand touching her hips lightly when she stumbled over loose pebbles.

They entered his house, a great grey stone structure now dark with ivy and sea dampness. He showed her into his drawing room and left her. She sat, oddly grateful for the warmth of the flames which glowed in the large fireplace. She realized her helplessness. She felt now, meekly tender and wistfully desirous of affection, like a small child. She stood up and moved closer to the fire, staring deeply into the flames as though there existed in the snapping embers the peace of knowing which she wanted.

He entered the room dressed in dark trousers, a soft plaid shirt, and moccasins, walking again with an unnatural step. He walked to a buffet. "Bourbon?" he asked.

"Rye," she said.

He mixed the drinks and placed one in her hand, which he brushed against for just a moment. She was suddenly conscious of the surging desire to have his hands touch her, to press close to the great strength of his chest. They stood, both staring into the struggling shadows of the hearth. Time was lost in the soundless high chanting of vast emotions.

"I am sorry," he said. A log crackled loudly as if to shatter his words. He touched her hair gently with his fingers. "We have come together," he said. "We cannot deny that which engulfed us."

She turned and felt his arms encircle her. Words forced themselves to her lips: "I love you, John Damon."

"Yes," he said, and he held her closely to him and kissed her with the unleashed ferocity of repressed necessity, and the endless expanse of enigma and isolation, and the mocking dancing filaments of ageless pain.

THE FABLE: PART THREE

George Kirman stopped the car before *Gull Crest* and sat for a moment. The dark stone house which stood alone above the land on one side and the sea on the other seemed less defiant than before, as though it realized that it was no longer as a fortress sheltering a man from a world which isolated him though he could not alienate it. Kirman was aware that the realization was his alone. He was aware, too, that his love for Duonia was an unanswerable thing now as he had known it would be. There was no bitterness, no self-reproach. He knew John Damon and Duonia well enough to recognize that just as she was the only woman who could love Damon, she was the only woman Damon could love. And this entire situation had seemed unalterable, like the inevitable opening of a flower.

He stepped out of the car and mounted the steps. Duonia opened the door. "George," she said with a smile, "how wonderful to see you."

He kissed her lightly. "Hello, Russe." He entered the large drawing room and turned to her. "I hadn't really looked this far ahead," he said smiling.

"To what?"

"To your being here. Congratulations, my love. I couldn't be happier, unless of course, you'd married *me*."

"You're sweet, George. But give me your things, and do sit down, you fool."

"I will if you'll sit with me. Where's John?"

"In his study," she said as she walked to a hallway closet and then back into the drawing room. She smiled and pointed overhead.

"Listen," she said.

Kirman sat down and listened to a steady thudding back and forth across the floor of the room above; unceasing, powerful, as though a great caged beast paced across and back in the narrow confines of his cell. Then there was the dragging of a chair into place, and the rapid staccato of a typewriter. Then a moment of silence followed by the scraping back of the chair and again the pacing – persistent, methodical, restless, tormented.

"He's working on a new book," she said. "He's indefatigable." There was a deep love in her eyes. "We work together. I have my easels in the study by a lovely window. I do tremendous amounts of work when I'm with him. I seem to absorb some of his torrent of impetus.

"I'm happy, George. Happier than I've ever known I could be. There is no longer a fraudulent mediocrity about my life. He drives me. There is the complete intensity of not a wasted hour – that entirety of application to a world all of us have sought. In its half diligence as I knew it before, it was an indescribable torture; I was torn, divided. Now it's a torment placated by realization." She smiled. "No more mediocrity. He's relentless."

At that moment, John Damon entered the room, clad in old white sailing pants and a faded denim shirt open at the neck. A wide smile creased his face when he greeted Kirman. "George," he said, "damn you, why haven't you been about sooner? I expected you'd be the first to congratulate me."

George laughed as he shook Damon's hand. "I was broken hearted," he said. "I thought Russe was calling to propose to me. Rather, she called to tell me she'd been indiscreet enough to marry *you*. But seriously, John, the best."

"Thanks, George," Damon said, and his eyes were full and embracing upon Duonia. He motioned for Kirman to be seated. He stood near the fireplace as Duonia brought them drinks.

31

"Shoal," Kirman said and they drank.

"I'm working on *The Egoism of the Race*," he said. He shuffled through some fifty odd pages of manuscript which he held in his hand. "I've got the nucleus and I'm building it forward. I'm using something I wrote years ago in *Burnt Umber*." He read; "'They live primarily under the impetus of their genius and encircle their lives by ignorance.'

"I become angry, George, very angry. The world has come to worship tawdry brilliance. I know not why, for I can trace but insatiate futility in it. I do know how; one has only to follow the increasingly universal effects of a striving of ease and material opulence. They are the barren criteria, the pervasive ideals. Connotatively, faith has been placed in objects, and the objects have returned a like faith – one of speed and efficiency in a mechanically circumvented life, one of industrial reliability bereft of imagination or sensitivity.

"There is such a paucity of self- interpretation by man. Ideals exist, as they always have, as they must, by virtue of elemental basis. But they fluctuate at the hand of the pragmatic world; wrongly of course. Ideology intermittently exists in shadow, emerges, sinks again into gloom. Such is our present aura; men have not realized the functional aspect of the pragmatic world and have allowed it to permeate their very souls.

"Even the element of personal freedom – with its tangents of integrity and independence, and so on – is non-existent. There are cries of communism, democracy, or monarchy; man today lives on the man of a single universal mechanocracy."

"So," Kirman said, "you censure industrialism, too."

"Yes," Damon said, "since it has had a more complete and definitive effect. Yet I do so in somewhat of a negative manner for it can only be positive through the absence in man of astute integration. Previous impedimenta to freedom were, almost exclusively, minority cliques with power; now the impediment is a universal which touches insidiously the being of the smallest man and which has the revolting hue of materialistic acquisition above and beyond else. Intangibles are even attributed to a harsh realm now.

"And I become angry over the fact this this generation is given over to pessimism of a dark sort which they will pass on – a bad inheritance. They stand in a maze of their own choice and, lost, bet their woe on such pitiably lisping tongues.

Why has there been so little real art in recent years? Simply because there is only the most dilute concentration in that so fine and crystal-like plain. It is all derivative; there are and have been swift and innumerable philosophic alterations and thence a result and indecision out of preoccupations with transients. And the path of least mental resistance delivers them to an expanse of stagnant fen."

"I agree," Kirman said. "Full thought is too arduous for them. I find it damned difficult to conceive halting as far short of fruition as they do. Their world is half grown."

"Yes," Damon said. "And that half-grown-ness, that adolescence, is the condemnation. From it there are derived the repeated or continuous manifestations of unexplored potential; from it stems the cultural, artistic, the truly valuable world's, call it what you will, dwarfism of today.

"Man is born inarticulate. That is the torture of creation. He must learn expression of even the most simple things. Thought can't exist unless a man can express it to himself; so a child's world is all animal reaction. The pain of such a process of learning is basic; so – if it is perpetuated to its end – is its ultimate base, a lucid essence? They do not approach lucidity; they do not know clarity. Art is the fullest awareness; and a paradox circles about it – that beauty is lost and becomes more lost to them.

"So much human perversion, if they could simply entertain the reasonability of it. In art again, the very command of order, the systemic harmony indicates simplified universals by way of selective truths. It is a reduction to basics in a way, if you follow me. And, physiologically – if an analogy may be drawn – man's most eloquent and true cry is emitted before some physically unkind or overly kind stimulus; there is little vagueness. So it is with art. It is similar to a straining of flesh for something; it must have the thing for which it grasps yet must tear itself from to reach its finality. And it must reach even further. Art is almost like sex."

The two men spoke together into the hours of night of the prodigious works of John Damon and the small attempts of Kirman. Kirman listened with Duonia to the man who remained an enigma, who wrote of tenderness and brutality and love and hate in a single hue, who touched the unseen hearts of men with his sensitivity, and who, as though he embraced too much, remained alone but for the gentleness of Duonia to whom he would always be a stranger.

As Damon spoke, he sat forward in his chair, his eyes wide and intense, his face animated. His words were hurried, those of a man pacing speech with speed of thought, attempting to create by his words the fleet, illusive images and subtle wraiths which crowded through his mind. At times he would rise, go to the piano, and play as though no one was present – perhaps Beethoven or Schumann, or perhaps one of his own – tormented, yet carrying in its full wildness and undeniable lyric quality which must live in a man of belief.

It was very late when Kirman left. After he had gone, Damon turned to Duonia. "I am going to work for a time."

"Let me remain up with you."

"I wanted you to say that. Stay up with me." He kissed her. "Nothing must ever happen to you. Life for me would stop."

"I love you, John."

"I know. I know, and yet each time you say it is to hear it again for the first time. I want you to say it."

"I want to say it again and again."

He took her in his arms and carried her upstairs to the study. She sat at his feet, her head resting against his leg as he wrote. She recalled his words, *glistening webs drawn out of darkness and damp shadow.* She wished to paint but the pounding of the typewriter lulled her to doze against his knee.

He lifted her to the studio couch and covered her gently, and stood watching her, an almost feminine tenderness on his face.

Light is not for us the night of children. We are old beyond our years and sleep is not a softening place in time. It is for us but a dark mirror of our day's turmoil and each new light must bring again, as well as its own, the rising ancient pains of others.

Then, in the dimness of the room, he lay down beside her fully clothed, put his arms about her, and slept.

THE FABLE: PART FOUR

The months of their marriage grew into two years – years fertile with the realization of their dedication to one another, pregnant with the wealth of their accomplishments.

And there were the times of their play: voyages up and down the coast in Damon's thirty-five-foot sloop, long peaceful evenings of concerts and good theatre, or at the less peaceful but interesting gatherings at Mitchell's. Often they merely descended the precipitous path behind *Gull Crest*, their home, to the secluded beach. There, blissful, they would be together and alone for hours of their choice. Having overcome the currents of the sea, they would run on the sand then he would lie beside her, both of them laughing. They felt the comforting rays of the sun warm on their bodies, fearless of the prudery opinions and eyes of an apprehensive world. He would rest his head against her smooth thighs and touch her flesh as something fragile and unreal, and they would speak into the soft breeze from the sea.

The morning of January 18th dawned through a sullen grey mist. Duonia and John sat on the studio couch drinking coffee and watching darkness decimate before the fulsome half-light of the dreary haze. He was more restless than usual. His hand trembled as he held his cup, his eyes roved nervously over the dull seascape which spread before them through the windows.

Duonia pressed her fingers tightly to his.

He turned to her. "I feel strangely today. There's a feeling of tremulous anticipation in me." He stood and walked to the French doors which opened upon a small balcony. He pulled them in and stood there, leaning against the door jamb, the wind ruffling his hair and billowing the tapestries which hung by the entrance.

Duonia went to him and took his hand in both of hers. She felt the quivering of his body. She looked at his face. A deep frown creased his forehead. His eyes were dark, nearly hidden behind his heavy brows as he stared, brooding, out over the white-streaked swells and into the distance of impenetrable mists. Waves crashed powerfully against the beach, thundered spray against the headlands to north and south.

She heard a faint sob stop in Damon's throat. His fingers tightened about her hands forcing a cry of pain to her lips. He turned to her, his arms hard about her, his mouth savagely pressed to hers. She felt her lips bruised against her teeth, tasted the sea moisture, acrid, on his lips. He carried her to their room.

Duonia lay still, breathing rapidly, shaking in the wake of violent exertion, and watched him dress. An unfamiliar sensation held her motionless, speechless, as though she had been suspended between two conflicting worlds.

There was a peculiar smile about Damon's lips as he drew on his garments – one of deep restrained joy, of defiantly accepted challenge.

He stood at the foot of the bed.

Duonia looked into his eyes and felt fear leap up to unfamiliar heights. She did not speak.

"I'll be going for a bit of sailing," he said, his fingers gentle on her ankle. "The air is good. I should be back before evening." Then he pressed his lips to the instep of her foot, as though he felt afraid to approach her closer, and he left.

Duonia went to the balcony outside the study and stood there. The light rain cold on her body, she watched him go. He turned and waved as he swung out past the sheltering headlands then hunched over the wheel. The south-east wind forced the boat over and he disappeared in the low-hanging clouds.

THE FABLE: PART FIVE

"George?"

"Russe, good to….."

"George, come to the house, will you?"

"What's the matter, Duonia? What's happened?"

"John's gone sailing."

"In this lousy weather? What's th…"

"George, please come up," she cried in a strangled voice. "I can't explain what I feel. Please."

"Okay, try to calm down a bit, sweet. Damon can sail a boat anywhere, you know that."

"I know, I know. But there's a terrible storm moving down the coast; I've heard the forecasts from Point Arena. Pressure is lower than it's been in years. Winds are hurricane velocity. Please, George, hurry."

"Yes, of course. I'll be there as soon as possible, about two hours. See you then."

THE FABLE: PART SIX

They stood on the cliff and waited, Duonia braced against a boulder, George Kirman with his feet planted wide apart, body thrust forward before the violent wind and driving rain. Kirman pointed his binoculars seaward. "Can't see a damn thing through these," he shouted. She nodded as they both protected their eyes with their hands and peered out at the raging sea.

With insane fury and multiple shrieks of wind, heavy black swells thudded over the rock headlands and seethed into the small bay.

Mountainous waves crashed over the boathouse, smashing it against the cliffs. Great plumes of spray leaped to where they stood and drove salt-immersed foam cruelly to their faces.

Duonia and Kirman trembled before the terrifying madness thrashing below them. Each envisioned the sloop helpless in the whipped spume.

Suddenly Kirman grasped Duonia's arm, stumbled as he did so then regained his balance in the wind. "He's coming," he shouted, pointing north-west.

They both stared into the rain, hands cupped about their eyes. "There!" he shouted.

The small craft rose for a moment on the crest of a great swell then vanished again from sight. They watched intently as it came closer." He's rolled and slashed his mainsail," Kirman said.

Duonia nodded and smiled, suppressing a desire to laugh joyously. The boat rose and fell, lost among the turbulent seas.

Then they could see him again, half crouched in the stern, one arm grasping the wheel, the other clutching the rigging as he handled the torn sheet. The craft was almost directly in front of them, drifting rapidly, turning slightly shoreward as Damon struggled to beach it.

"The drift!" Kirman shouted. "The damn drift!"

The boat was born relentlessly down on the southern rocks. They saw Damon grappling with the canvas and the rudder. Kirman watched, feeling helpless and yet entranced; Duonia screamed yet could not look away. Then Damon loosened his grasp on the sail, stood for a moment in the pit, and leaped into the water. Seemingly unconquerable, indefatigable, his great arms drove him through the seas. They watched, horrified as he sank in the troughs, rose on the frothing crests, disappeared for interminable moments to reappear as though indestructible.

Swimming steadily, carried by a heavy roller, he was lifted against a high conical rock. Duonia screamed again. The wave passed over him. He clung there as if stunned, without moving. Suddenly he clamored upward, out of reach of the water, and crouched as he watched the broken remains of the sloop being pounded against the reefs. He turned and waved to them. They waved back.

"He's safe," George said. "Safe for you, Duonia."

"Yes," she said, "he's safe." And she wept.

And as she spoke the words, as if in mockery, a tremendous wave advanced, as if it was the entire sea, insurmountable, destructive. It roared its final challenge in a crazed frenzy – rushed toward the rock. Titan depth. Wrathful brute. Devouring.

They watched in speechless horror. Damon saw it as they did. He turned directly toward it, faced the plunging giant, surging terror there, and sat, waiting. Heaving, dynamic, silent force, it reached him; he stood to his full height, poised slightly forward, waved to them again and dove into engulfing darkness. He was smashed against the base of the cliffs.

Duonia hid her face against George's jacket. Dry-voiced she said, "It almost doesn't seem that he existed."

"No," George said holding her close. "Perhaps we've been dreaming and dreamt of the God of Things."

Duonia felt again the great pain – her splintered heart, the bruises on her body, and wondered if she was alive or back there in the lashing sea.

THE MOUNTAIN SHADOW

Gaya is a farmer, a man of God and peace. All farmers are men of God and peace. Work in the earth is Gaya's God and his sanctity, he lives with the soil. The earth never leaves him. There is always the fresh earth smell on his body. It is under his fingernails even as he splashes his thick, blunt hands in the well near his hut. It is under the fingernails of his soul and it does not leave him. He husbands the moist loam. He knows it. He treats it when it is ill and impoverished as one treats an ailing child. He has his farm, and his wife: Gurka, wife of Gaya, a large woman, strong. He husbands her as he does his earth. There is compassion, an affection. They step, one foot on the turned-soil-ridge, the other in the furrow, broken-legged fashion. No one speaks of love. Their words are in the conversation of their togetherness and the rhythmic bending of the back with the sowing of each seed.

All has beginning and ending here for them – each hour so much bending and so much reaping. Days are without number and years fall, almost without counting, like rain in the field of their lives. They work and do not count the time, for time is fear and they do not like fear – it has no place in their living.

It is twilight. Gaya sits and watches the mountain shadow of night deepen. Dew falls; birds scuffle and settle in their nests. Gurka thumps the straw of the mat upon which she and her man have made six children. Ten years. The bed is good for them yet. The sons grow strong. Soon this land – she runs through it all in her mind; her life – Gurka, wife of Gaya.

Gaya dozes on his stool beneath the thatch eves in front of the hut. He wonders at the shadow and where the shadow goes. But a shadow is just a shadow across the earth.

A man shuffles out of the gloaming. He steps in the long free strides from the hip of a walker made to walk. He utters a greeting to Gaya, hesitates at the crude gate. "Yes, yes, come in. Welcome." Gaya gestures and the man leaps the fence lightly, drops his coat to the grass, and sits. He reaches for a curve-stemmed pipe and a tobacco pouch in his shirt. The dust of many roads is on him and there is a casualness in his actions, a brightness in his eyes, and yet, a long, deep gaze.

"It is a good evening is it not, friend?"

"Yes, farmer, a good evening."

"You travel far?"

"Travel is always far." He turns more toward Gaya and draws deeply of his pipe, the faint smoke reaching for the sky.

Gaya stamps the tobacco more firmly into the bowl of his clay pipe with the end of his thumb and listens, observing the lengthening shadow. The wanderer takes some earth in his hand and begins to speak. "This is good land, farmer. You have good crops?"

"Yes," says Gaya, "good crops."

"At times there is envy in me for men like you." The walker's eyes rove over the plowed fields in mixed longing and disdain. "To have one love, a single heart, and then to sow each seed of love and to reap your harvest and know its fullness must bring great satisfaction."

Gaya nods. This stranger is right; he mouths good words. A rich content is in the breast of Gaya. He feels anew and affection for his land and smiles at the heavy, peaceful tiredness in his body. He turns to the man. "But you wander? Why? Why do you wander?"

The man draws on his pipe. "Distance is a virtue of the world and a man's feet made to walk. Dissatisfaction breeds often in the loam of one place. I, now, can banish my unrest in new distance, never allowing fermentation, for there is disquiet within men of your ways. It is a frail thing in most as is a delicate green shoot in a tended garden. But at times it grows, and, as in an earth ill-fostered there exists a random growth with perchance an adder coiled within the mat, so men become ill-tempered and live a clouded trauma of resentment and self-reproach. Life about them is a girth, and those nearby notice that they do not smile. They are divided men. Too young they defeat or too long they wait.

"You watch the shadow now; it tops the rise there, slowly, and you wonder: your piece of ground, what other grains of earth are of it, what other man walks there and what seeds sown, and what winds do blow?

"So I partake of varied realms, never allowing myself the thought that my life might be better lived elsewhere and plied at other tasks. My air is free and each man's soil is mine. I do not get to know something so that I get to love it, for to love is to know hate and I do not choose to hate, and one is not without the other. My living is a less complicated thing and in its simplicity time is not a burden. Hours fall as leaves and I know the shuffling through them and the sound is not unkind and not without a quaint ironical humor. When I laugh I am not certain in my laughter that I must weep. My soul sees through many eyes."

Gaya searches the face of the stranger. "But what of loneliness?"

"Loneliness is a strange woman with whom all men sleep yet of whom few partake. And mind you, farmer, she has pleasure, a bewildering pleasure perhaps, but to sleep beside and know her and not fear her – that is her greatest seduction. And all women are destined to hurt one time, so..." He shrugs away his smile and casts the dying embers of his pipe among the shadowed blades of grass, and then he goes on. "There are other things. No use to say, but no longer do I know wherein lies faith. It is not of my knowing or my concern. You are a tenant; your living is your concern."

The words burn deep in Gaya's heart as he feels an inner looseness like swirling dust. "I like the earth. I like it moist and firm. I make it good. I live with it and plants grow. I love the feel of it crumbling in my hands. I know it here." He strikes his chest. "It is firm, kind. The world is dark. I do not know it. The moist earth is mine. I like it damp and wet. I hate the tortured look of dry dirt torn by winds. We carry buckets, my woman and I, and it is damp..."

Gurka calls. Gaya stirs and rubs his eyes. His brow is creased.

"What is it, Gaya?" She moves over to make space for him on the mat.

42

"I had a – a dream."

"Yes?"

"Yes."

WILD PARROT'S FLIGHT

PART I:

The sun had not yet taken the frost from the leaves and grasses. Its rays pushed in slanted beams through morning fogs and swamp mists, and a dark mosaic of shadow lay across the earth. Birds flew far, occupied with morning's forage; it was still but for an occasional sparrow chirping and rustling in the brush, or the remote crow of a rooster.

Mellie stirred in bed and turned to bury her face into Booker's neck. She felt only the warmth of where he had lain and she remembered. She heard his voice again telling her, as he was leaving for the mill, to remain in bed until the sun took away the morning chill. She sighed with pleasure, stretched languorously, then rolled into the place where he had slept. She curled her body against the blankets where there lingered the faint odor of him. She remembered the night; she didn't want to get up. To get up was to be alone and she lay still and smiled in memory: Mrs. Booker Harmon – she turned the name over in her mouth and felt the wonder of it. Glad to be young, glad to be with Booker. She could smile at everything and think of nothing else. She hugged her arms tightly about her breasts and knew that Booker would be home in the evening.

Having dozed she was startled by the cluck of a hen and looked about the room. The hen stood just inside the door, regarding the dim interior with head cocked to one side. Mellie laughed; she threw back the covers quickly, sat up, and put her feet on the earth floor. The hen fluttered out, cackling wildly.

Mellie rubbed the sleep from her eyes. She sat quietly, her hands gently caressing her rounded belly. "Lil' Booker," she said. "Ev'rythin's alright, honey. Yoah papa an' me, we's married. Ev'rythin's alright." She reached for the faded gingham dress and slipped it over her head, still talking softly. "But then, yo' mus' feel it in me, Lil' Booker, 'cause you's in theah, too. Lawd yes, yo mus'." She walked to the table and ate the grits she'd prepared the night before, then she thought of the room and of cleaning and of its being her home and Booker's. She wanted to sit quietly and feel the sweet fullness in her, but she roused herself. She carried water from the well to wash the few dishes, made the bed, arranged the table and chairs, cleaned the old stove, brought in kindling for a fire, and, in between, sat down to take from her her happiness, to look at it and turn it over, then to put it back and feel it welling deep and strong inside her. She began to sing as she swept:

"Oh th' rooster's outa bed and the hen's all fed an' ah ain' goin' a worry no mo-ore."

She left off the words and hummed the familiar tune, smiling as she worked, the thing too great and full in her to remain unnoticed. She paused now and then to hold a laugh of joy. "Mah man," she said. "Ah ain' goin' a worry no more."

The hours of morning passed sluggishly, hours composed of minutes which fell one upon the other with hateful regularity and slowness. Mellie sat and counted them, eagerness in her heart, excitement out-running time and returning, then going ahead of it again. Thoughts of herself and Booker excluded all and the pleasures of the night before were reborn again and again.

Toward eleven o'clock she prepared Booker's lunch. He'd told her she could meet him near the mill on the other side of the swamps. "Folla th' road aroun' th' bogs, honey," he had said. "Ah'll meet yo half way an' we kin eat t'getha. Don' go through th' swamps. Ah'll teach yo about 'em soon an' then yo' can." But now it was only eleven or so and that meant she would have to wait until past noon before leaving. Mellie laughed as she thought of his surprise if she was waiting outside of the mill.

She wrapped the food in a handkerchief, brushed her hair, tied it back with a piece of wrapping cord and wound a few daisies into its black fullness.

Humming, with the lunch under her arm, knowing there was no time to follow the road if she were to be waiting at the packer's entrance when he came out, she entered the swamp. It was still there in tangled foliage of cypress and oak and the pale gray Spanish Moss. The water lay stagnant, brackish and dark about her. It was mysterious and a fear seemed drawn tightly over it all. A quiet sense pervaded Mellie's being and worried her step. She chose from among the paths and went slowly where she feared quicksand. The heat was oppressive, a dead heat coming up from the stagnant water and held low over foul earth by the close-matted canopy overhead. Perspiration dampened Mellie's body and prickled her scalp, and her breathing came more quickly though she walked slowly and with caution. Time passed with careful steps over each doubtful spot and with the confusion of conjecture over the earth's secureness. At moments she wished she hadn't come. She wondered how late it was. It seemed she'd been walking for a great time, choosing trails, going deeper into the gloom of the bog – ground and brush.

And then suddenly she was out of the entanglement of the fen and on the dusty road.

Shadows told her that it was past twelve. She looked back at the swamps then decided to go to the mill by way of the road. She quickened her pace. Booker would be coming that way and she thought of his great frame swinging lithely along. She hurried her steps, anxious to be with him.

She did not meet him on the road. She had wasted too much time in the swamp. She became angry at herself for having gone contrary to Booker's instructions. Heavy at heart thinking that he had no lunch, she went on with an uncertain, distressful feeling.

The dust of the road was hot to her feet when she arrived at the mill. She asked an older white man near the door of the store-shed, if she could see Booker Harmon, and she waited, standing on a patch of short grass.

The man disappeared into the darkness of the building and returned in a few moments. "He ain't here. You his wife? He left over an hour ago t' meet cha. He ain't come back yet. Should a been here long ago."

Mellie frowned and left, hurrying back through the warm dust of the road. *Must a gone home lookin' f' me*, she thought, and she was afraid of his anger now. She didn't want to make his gentle voice hard, and she didn't want to fear him.

Before she looked up to see her home, she noticed the imprint of his feet in the dust. He was home, she thought. She ran through the door. "Booker, honey, it's me," she said. "Ah got to ---- Booker?"

She was alone. She left the lunch on the table and looked about, confused, perplexed. His blue denim jacket was on the hook by the bed. She went to the door and noticed that his footprints led, with the ones she had formerly made, into the swamp. Panicked, she called out and followed them, running, anxious to overtake him. She slowed to a walk, out of breath, tears streaming down to her lips, losing the marks in the glade region and finding them again in the soft mud and losing them again. It grew late and her body was tired. Her legs ached from uneven walking – she turned home. She would not go again to the mill. She would be waiting when he came home.

PART II:

As he crossed the yard Booker noticed the small footprints which led from the door of his shack to the swamp. A brief spasm of fear gripped him. He called out, "Mellie, w'ere are ya, honey?" But he didn't expect an answer. His vague hope and the silence covered him in a real fear before he called.

He entered and looked about. He saw where she had prepared his lunch. She had gone then, to meet him. But through the swamps! He was filled with great tenderness and love, and a half-anger out of his deep fear. He left his jacket and rushed down the dark trail, his great voice echoing through the morass, ringing his desperation and anguish to the cypress and oak, to the fetid, placid water which seemed to mock his dread. He ran, his heavy chest rising and falling rapidly, rivulets of perspiration channeling the tan dust which had come from the road. He cursed his oneness when he came to a choice of paths and then plunged on, hoping to his God that he'd chosen the correct one. He ran to the large quicksand pits first, afraid not to. His voice became harsh with calling; sweat trickled through his eyebrows into his eyes, burning, blurring vision. "Th' pit," he said. "Mah lord gawd, ah gotta go t' th' pit." He stumbled, slipped as he jumped to a bog. He thought of the sand and of those who'd fallen there. He ran on, swearing in soundless sobs at the boughs which whipped his face. Then he reached the treacherous patch, its evil, light brown surface at his feet. His voice broke the stillness in great sobbing gusts. He swayed drunkenly and put his hands to his eyes. A patch of black hair was barely visible on the tan, solid earth-appearing surface. "Mah gawd," he cried. "Mah lord gawd, Mellie! Mellie!"

His wild cries echoed through the stillness of the place. He threw himself to the ground, attempting to reach the hair, talking incoherently out of his torture and anguish, roaring like a crazed beast against the injustice which clawed weakly, fiercely in him. He could not reach it. He broke brush boughs frantically and threw them on the quicksand. He took off his trousers and tied one leg to a tree root and with the other leg crawled out on the boughs. He began to sink. The bending branches slipped slowly off. He reached for the hair, tried to battle the clutching suction of the pit.

The sand claimed slowly, was to his armpits before he would recognize the effort was futile. He pulled on the trousers, his strong body trembling. He felt the cloth tear and again his powerful voice disturbed the quiet of the swamp, and there was silence. There was the unruffled water, the fluttering whir of a wild parrot's flight, and nothing more.

PART III:

Mellie lay still on the bed, anticipation frail and trembling within her delicate, rapid heartbeat. She stared at the ceiling. A smile played across her lips and now and then a gentle laughter, and again the sober smile of peaceful, happy contemplation. A spider dropped from the rafters to her breast. She laughed softly and watched him, liking the sensation of his tiny body moving over her bare flesh. And then she brushed him away; she wished he was there again then turned her thoughts to Booker.

Afternoon shadows moved across the floor and started up the wall; hours passed with hours earlier, and so she waited.

Around six o'clock the men from the mill began to straggle by. Mellie heard their laughter at jokes about one another, listened to the overall hum of their conversation. She waited to hear Booker's deep voice above the others, but she did not hear him and she stood, dressed, and went to the door. She asked for him.

He hadn't returned to work following the noon hour. "We tho't he was with yo'," they said and passed on.

She stood and watched them go. She became worried. A faint anguish filled her and magnified itself until her heart pulsed in a void of terror. She felt weak.

Sol and Gadger stopped by and, in her desperate loneliness and fear she told them of her anxiety, yielding to the urge to confide in someone familiar and consoling. The swamp, she told them, he had gone into the swamp.

"Now, Mellie girl," old Gadger said, "Ah wouldn't fret none ovah Booker ef I was yo', but me'n Sol, we'll have a look t' please yo'."

They turned into the swamp from the road and Mellie went with them. They walked a way through the marsh and heavy foliage and then heard voices ahead of them on the close trail; they stopped. A group of mill workers came through the brush. "We got Booker, Sol," one said, and he became still when he saw Mellie. "An Esther, too," a voice from behind said, and someone told the voice to shut up. "We foun' 'em in th' pit," the first said quietly.

The bodies were set down and the men stood quietly as if waiting.

Mellie sobbed for a moment – a vacant, dead sob, hard and torn, and she put a hand on old Gadger's shoulder. Her other hand pressed to the roundness of her belly. "Booker," she said, and her voice was hardly audible. She looked at Esther for a long time, and then back at Booker, and then she turned and ran wildly into the shack.

"Y' bettah take Booker to my place," old Gadger said, "an take *her* to Mis' Lil's place. She's made 'nuff bus'ness there. An y' bettah tell Ju Ju, somebody." The men moved off with their burdens. Old Gadger turned to look at the shack and heard Mellie's sobbing and shook his head then went slowly down the road.

PART IV:

Three days later, two wagons left the town. Ju Ju drove alone on one and went out through the north flats.

Sol drove the other, out to the cemetery. Old Gadger sat behind him on a large plank seat, holding Mellie whose eyes were dry and whose face was tired and drawn. Some others followed and the wagon creaked and bounced, and the rough pine box jolted against the backboard.

PART V:

The late afternoon sun probed into the dimness of the room as though to shutter the pall of desolateness, but Mellie was unaware. The bed curled itself gently about her as if offering solicitude. Its warmth was incongruent. She rose from the bed and lay down on the long bench and stared passively at the ceiling, apathetic, weak before the anguish which seemed as a dead thing. Her hands were crossed dumbly on her breast. She lay quietly, her body trembling occasionally before the deep grief, her teeth clenching, her head rolling from side to side. She could not understand: *Why?* pounded in her mind like a woman's hands beating against the great gray blocks of a prison cell. Then she would lie quietly again and think, and recall the child which was forming slowly in her belly, and she was bitter, a hurt wrinkling her brow, tightening her eyes, and she clenched wildly at her slightly rounded stomach in fierce desire to tear the shapeless thing from her. Then bitterness out-shadowed grief. She envisioned Booker's tall, strong form, and then Esther, Esther with Booker, Esther who called men from the second story window of a shabby gray building, who spoke to men on the street and beckoned them to follow her through the sagging door of *Mis Lil's Place*. No! No! Her body convulsed from within and she sagged back limply and thought of Booker's tenderness, the great hard strength of his being, the merciless joyous pressure of his body, his strong sureness. She pressed each line of her body to the rigid coldness of the bench and smiled wistfully for a moment, and then the bitterness came back, slowly, admitted reluctantly, demanding. A deep and wailing curse smothered itself in her and she lay quietly again and still, staring mutely at the idly waving cobwebs, gray shadows among the rafters.

PART VI:
Days later, Mellie lay less within the pall of uncertainty and insecurity. Her throat ached from the goiter of bitterness and disillusionment which clung there. Her jaw tightened, her eyes remained expressionless, and her lips drew back in a hard and false smile. She walked about aimlessly, shrouded by a haunting and inexplicable enigma. She went through the north flats and looked at the poorly marked grave and laughed with a harsh voice. She left slowly and walked back into town.

PART VII:
Just before the sun went down, at about eight o'clock, the men from the fields north of the mill began to trickle down the road. Mellie stood in the doorway, dress unbuttoned low, and watched them and smiled. "It's Booker's wife," they said and laughed. Three young ones entered the yard and passed through the door – Mellie turned and followed them.

ACROSS LEAGUELESS SPACE.

Caraway sat back supinely. His left hand held his drink, toyed with it absently running the bottom of the glass in circles over the arm of the chair. His right hand conveyed a cigarette intermittently to his lips. Other than that, his portly body did not move.

Hartney watched Caraway's left hand. The stout, short fingers seemed as though they might lose control of the glass. They did not. They continued the manipulation gracefully, strongly, apparently without effort. The gesture was significant to Hartney. But there was no other movement of significance. The action of the right hand was defined, expressionless, consisting of smoke and habit. Even Caraway's eyes, usually alert and alive in his heavy face, were inexpressive, staring into the shadow of the room and across leagueless space.

Hartney glanced at Dick Lieber. Lieber was engrossed in the smoke from his cigarette, watching as it rose and dispersed in a preoccupied manner. He was silent. Dick never said much. He listened and nodded agreement as dissent and remained silent. Stillness could become awkward and yet he would say nothing, would remain unperturbed, would seem oblivious and detached, indifferent to conversational necessity. He would merely wait as he waited now. At such moments he aggravated Hartney.

Hartney turned from him and back to Caraway. He watched the glass for a moment. "Why are you studying, Buff?"

"For the hell of it," Caraway said without moving. "Why are *you*?"

"I'll use a hackneyed phrase," Hartney said. "I suppose it's what the philosophers have called…"

"Truth?" Caraway said. He laughed. "God, hackneyed?" He stopped toying with his drink. "The phrase has been raped. Other abortions aside, you people don't even differentiate between truth and logic any longer. Perhaps never did."

"Do you?" Hartney asked.

Caraway stood up and walked to a window. He opened it. "Come here," he said.

Hartney rose and went to his side.

"There's your truth," Caraway said and pointed to the street and out over the maze of buildings and alleys – a labyrinth of shadow and feeble yellow light from streetlamps and flapping clothes hanging in backyard blackness. "There's your truth," he said again. "Everything that exists, everything that has form or life or both, that's truth. Each thing out there supplements and is supplemented by every other thing." He closed the window and sat down again.

Hartney poured a drink then took his chair.

Caraway propped his feet on a footstool and stared between them. "Existence is truth, not fabrication or shadow or dreams. The ultimate of the world is truth. It is body and body is life and therefore undeniable. Truth does not differentiate; it is organization. Logic is what draws angles and not parallels to existence. Logic distinguishes beauty from sordidness, harmony from confusion. Logic warns, it takes truth and draws angles of divergence and is directive of thought to the often elusive intangibilities of right and of loveliness, of the golden ideal, which so often is merely self-terminating and thereby weak. But that's your distinction."

Hartney sipped his drink and smoked. "What do you believe in?"

"What do you mean?" Caraway asked.

"Religion," Harney said, "or just faith?"

"What church do you go to?"

"Catholic."

"You ought to distinguish between religion and faith," Caraway said.

"Do you?" Hartney asked.

"No," Caraway said. "I believe in the relativity of all things, and that all are divisible in part by all else. My faith is in the equation and in the quotient result. Mine, I suppose, is a philosophy of equanimity, a recognition of existence. But I do not justify. If I don't like a result, I try to alter it. If I can't, I live with it. I've lived with things not liked before.

"But the church exculpates; it has to. It teaches first an avoidance of truth's mutations. It avoids the immediate by ethereal concentration. People are affected poignantly by reality so the church has convenient rationalizations among its doctrines. But sometimes disunity results, a blurred focus. It comes of a fallacy in the church's method of teaching. It has attempted to fuse ideology of the theological sort with pragmatism. No ideology can be fussed with pragmatism. The end is a confusion, a phase of disunity; people have to choose. They have a time of it for they are not disconnected. The church has reminders to obscure, or attempt to, that fact. Some fall before the half-plans. The result of that is disillusionment."

"Disillusionment is resultant of frailty," Hartney said.

"No," Caraway said. "Disillusionment is difficult; it is composite." He gestured as he talked now, with his glass and with his cigarette. "It is never one thing. The mind collapses many things in such a disposition. Even strong minds which fail to recognize the relationship of things, and cause and effect, the divisors, enter the shadow and become the incongruent members of society, the disunified." Caraway stood and mixed a drink. "I can tell you a story."

Lieber nodded.

"Go ahead," Hartney said.

Caraway sat down again and lit a cigarette and regarded for a moment the yellow stain on his fingers. "This is a story of many things. It is a composite: it is of disillusionment and, more predominantly, a story of the deposition of a pattern. It is of Mark and Isabelle.

"Mark and I went to grammar school together and later to high school. We came to know one another pretty thoroughly through those years but our friendship remained a frail affair. He was sensitive, more so than I, and whereas I was almost inarticulate, his words, both written

54

and spoken, were alive and poetic and advanced. The poet was alive even then, and I admired him. A barrier was thereby created and we were somewhat estranged.

"His sensitivity was fortunate in him. His family was more than comfortable financially and their summers, as he recounted them, sounded periods of paradise to me. He drew from those summers by way of essays and young verse and I worshipped such visions as he created. I suppose it was rather a worship by me of him, by one pitiably impoverished before such things for one rich and noble in them. Whatever it was, envisioning those things through him engendered first desires in me. I was cloddishly slow in forming but soon we ran closely parallel during those four years of high school. We became close out of varied mutualities exclusive of writing, and our lives developed harmony. It is there that the story begins.

"Mark's poetry was his life. His devotion to it was completely ardent. His thought was delicately sensitive and finely balanced and manifested itself in various forms of verse. It foretold greatness.

"Such a man is recognized and becomes a promontory toward which people direct themselves with a certain restraint and remoteness. For one so young and possessed of such sensitivity that loneliness became a strong and demanding shadow. He required release other than mute, unresponsive sheaves of paper for these were multitudes of enigmas and dogmas which shook themselves through his mind. He found such release in two people: Isabelle and me.

"I was more of an objective factor in his life than subjective. I suppose most relationships of man to man are predominantly objective, but no matter. Our words were many. I came to know him far beyond any point wherein he could know himself. He was possessed of many fears and presentiments, and those often constituted the speech of our hours together.

"Respecting the medium towards which he was directed, I was afraid that his fears would be conducive to restrictive philosophies. I attempted to make him recognize the relative mien of things, the inevitable causes and effects. He could not. He was too emotional, too hypersensitive to foster such rationality. Such men as he when they incorporate wisdom do so in an almost mystic manner, sensing rather than deducing by any definite process. But some element of Mark's nature was too young to maintain equanimity of itself. He deposed whatever universality he might have embraced by strongly adopting religious bent.

"Then he met Isabelle. I hoped that she might epitomize what faith he needed. However, he was too far gone and, unable to avoid the one, he held to both. And as with anything he loved, and it became love in both instances, he embellished each in the fine flowing language which was his. All of his poetry was either religious in nature or lauded love and Isabelle. He loved her with a noble and dominating love which was one of the finest I've seen. And she idolized him. She became of his religion through him, and he was her faith.

"Nor did Mark love Isabelle merely out of reacting of male to female. That was impossible, for her very femininity was the ultimate of multiple things: her fine scholarly brain, her perception of hardly sensible issues, her apparently limitless compassion, and her extraordinary capabilities as a musician.

"And out of all that, she was woman enough not to embrace the arid aloneness of a singular life but to desire her converse in nature. Such a complementary tendency led her to great adoration of Mark. The mutual strength and vitality of their minds could hardly have been finer, but neither was cognizant of the fact of a balance of life, my rational realism.

"Time passed, and Mark's bent by the junior year was towards the ministry. At first I had set myself against that, yet, regardless of his deep feelings towards me, it was in vain. I realized early that it would be but could not desist until all ostensible results indicated my futility, for I knew at start that in such a case one cannot divert another's ways.

Such revolution must come from within. So we remained the closest of friends but of diverse philosophies.

"Passing years brought a war. We graduated school and became, with numerous others, fine pellets for the fishbowl. Isabelle, realizing his eligibility, insisted on marriage. But I believe Mark desisted because of what he felt so strongly within him. In his poetry I had always sensed presentiments of early fatality. I never said anything of them, always scoffed and condemned them as elements of his brooding artistry when he would phrase his fear. To Isabelle I would attempt to stabilize mood and annihilate anguish. I had become a father-confessor to both of them. It may seem strange, but we were young and striving to ascertain firm ground though our paths differed. As it developed, their path was of more infirm and treacherous nature than mine.

"Mark and I were drafted together and did basic together but later on our outfits changed. We saw action at the same time though on different fronts. I lost contact with him. Word came to me by way of another friend that Mark had been badly wounded in Belgium. I wrote to Isabelle several times. She answered once saying that…well, I have her letter here." Caraway got up and rummaged through an old box. He unfolded the letter and read:

"Dear Buff, I received your fine letter two days ago. I know I should have told you of Mark's injury but I've been busy attempting to discuss the extent of his hurt. We can get no information on that. We do know that he will be here in the States soon.

"You know how happy I shall be to have him near again. My dear Mark – it has been so long. I am counting each day until I can be near him again. He was….

"Well, she goes on at some length in reminiscences. I did not hear from her after that though I wrote repeatedly.

"Two years later I was discharged; about a year and a half ago, that is. I hunted up Mark as soon as I could. He was still stationed at an Army hospital in North Carolina but was home on furlough when I got to his place. His mother told me, before I met him again, not to mention Isabelle, that they hadn't seen her for some time. She also told me much of his wounds. A fifty-caliber machine gun had stitched him up the right side. A part of his skull was gone. 'He has trouble remembering,' she said.

"He was sitting in a chair when I entered the living room. He smiled when he saw me, extended his left hand, and cried. As I took it, I wanted to cry myself. I recalled his forebodings and wished he'd known them in actuality. His right leg was gone from above the knee, his right arm paralyzed, but that could have been accepted. He tried to speak to me. He groped for words, made gestures helplessly, and cried harder. I listened as he found a few words: *war...killing.* He shook his head. *Long time – bad.* He cried again. For the first time in my life I felt frantically helpless. I had difficulty finding the words myself. *Hospital,* he said, *doctors fix – head.* He indicated with his left hand a large hollow beneath the hair on the right side of his head.

"'Plate,' I'd said.

"'Yes...plate,' he'd said.

"We spoke for some time. I brought up people we knew and he frowned in attempt to recall them. 'Skinny – nice fellow – fun – yes,' he would say.

"I stayed for several hours and then left. I was angry. I thought of men I'd known who had lived whole and entire and who had little to give. I thought of myself. And then I thought of the fineness which had been Mark: shattered, irreparable to former standards, his greatness lost, and only a bruised hulk remaining. Mark grasping for words. They were sending him to rehabilitation classes to learn to speak. I was bitter.

"Everything was relative, divisible by every other thing. It was right, I knew that, but philosophy must be remote in such instances to be completely valid from a personalized view. I was too close to Mark. Time tempered and validified, however. And Mark's own actions – he committed suicide three months ago.

"And Isabelle? Well, Mark had become a cause. The war was not the effect. Cause and effect fall into arrangement only when those elements vitally embraced are included. Isabelle was the effect. With her the violence of a machine gun expended itself. I have some clippings, two to be exact."

Caraway passed them first to Hartney. They were from *The New York Record*, sectioned City Court.

Arraigned on charges of lascivious carriage, drunkenness, and disturbing the peace, Miss Isabelle Webb, Queens.

The second appeared of a date four months later in the same section. *Arraigned on charges of lascivious carriage and soliciting for immoral purposes; Miss Isabelle Webb, Bronx.*

Caraway got up and mixed himself another drink. Hartney passed the clippings to Lieber.

"Truth?" Hartney asked.

"Truth," Caraway said. "But truth doesn't make distinctions. Logic does." He paused with the shaker in his hands. "But if I could have told them, would it have made any difference?"

WRAITHS IN THE NIGHT

Martin Hart relaxed against the rail of the *Manfren*. He swore to himself; he had wanted to be alone for a moment with the sea and the night, to know the affinity he felt with them. He was conscious now only of the girl who had joined him quietly, who stood beside him, her body warm against his, her head against his shoulder. He pressed his lips to the fragrance of her hair then he struck a match, held it to his cigarette, and flicked it down into the darkness. It disappeared in the luminescence of the bow wash. He drew smoke deep into his lungs and stared out over the gentle swells.

Marcia Wright reached into the pocket of his trousers, her hand pressed to his thigh. She took a cigarette and lit it. Her face was white in the darkness. The warm breeze lifted her hair back from her shoulders; it bellowed the folds of her light negligee about her like tongues of flame in the night.

"Why did you leave me?" she asked.

"I couldn't sleep. I came out for a cigarette."

"What time is it?"

"Four-thirty."

She walked to a low deck chair. "Let's sit here for a time." She waited until he sat down. She sat with him, her head on his chest, her legs curled beneath her, and looked out at the sea. She ran her slender fingers gently over his wrist.

I feel none of the tenderness she feels at this moment, Hart thought. *The paradox of need, perhaps.*

The ship rolled slightly. Wisps of cloud scudded across the sky, great moon-shadows noiseless over the swells, pale wraiths in the night.

"Tomorrow evening we'll be in the Java Sea," she said.

"Yes."

"What are you thinking, Mart?"

"I don't know. Primarily, I suppose, of the desperation which is over this beauty, for one is aware of transientness even as one observes. I suppose I was thinking too of the beauty itself, of how much I love all of this."

"Love *me,* Mart."

He carried her to her cabin.

That evening they gathered in the lounge of the *Manfren* as had been their custom since leaving Liverpool. They had come together by chance quite casually and continued to meet without appointment at the same table at the same time. They sat and smoked and drank port and told stories. They passed the hours of each afternoon talking vicariously of their varied orbits.

Berntzen, a pale-faced Belgian foreign-imports trader, was telling of a man in Shanghai. Martin Hart smoked silently, drank his port, and listened, aware that Marcia Wright was observing him from across the table, aware that no one suspected their intimacy, their love; aware, too, that Mrs. Berntzen, though smiling in acknowledgement of her husband's words, for some reason hated him.

Berntzen was interrupted as the steward gave the captain a dispatch. Everyone smoked in silence while Captain Moreson read and then scrawled his signature on the paper. The steward was dismissed. Moreson turned to the people at the table. "Typhoon coming up from the south. We shall be through the strait and in the lee of Java before she strikes this area. Sorry to interrupt."

"As I was saying," Berntzen continued, "this man, Bonguereau, now controls the jade exports of all China and two thirds of the cultured pearl industry of the Orient. That is a man with a Midas Touch, I think."

"A man I should like to meet," Jonathan Wright said with a nod of humor. "He might like my daughter."

"Father!" Marcia said.

"You might meet him," Berntzen said. "British Consul to Japan,

61

you might have to handle exports to your country. Bonguereau ships pearls from Yokohama." He winked at Marcia, "You might meet him, yes."

There was silence. Hart sipped his port slowly then began to speak. "You Belgians, for a small race, are certain. I have met your like before. I knew a man who was not so certain. I knew a man whose pursuits were less substantial than those of this trader of yours, Berntzen. In fact, the thing which drew him from normal loads and divorced him from the often peaceful common existence was so obscure as to be, much of the time, his pursuer. I don't believe he could have told by way of definition what his life meant. He was an amorphous creature molded of two worlds, drawn to one and, of a deep curiosity, to the other by virtue of humanisms strong within him. He was bound, powerless to take either world to exclusion of the other.

"One conceives of reconciliation, perhaps. I don't know. He attempted it once with a sort of desperate application. It failed. Marriage shared more darkly the line between and made of itself and its surroundings troublesome. He was not for it, for there was imposition. A man's life lost its unity; it became part of the life of another, and so a part of varied and numerous others. And slowly, very slowly, there developed relationships and obligations. Moments of aloneness were no longer possessed; they were purloined from the intricacies of a developing pattern and then, phantom-like, slipped away.

"He wondered at the enigma which magnified unrest in him and was aware only that he must move on and wait. He did not know why or for what it was that he waited. He knew merely that no person could subdue his desires or infringe upon his aloneness or cast about him enduring boundaries. And he knew that for some inexplicable reason he was powerless before it himself.

"There could be no variance with elements felt so strongly. He yielded to the lunging impetus of the world which denied him facile communion with most people. Occasionally he would reach back into

62

that other world wherein dwelt his other self and it was as if he were taking a small child by the hand.

"Few realized the turgidity, the deep intensity of isolation which clung about his being. He believed himself lost, born of some alien union. Yet I suppose his life had a definition, of which he rarely thought; one which led him from hemisphere to hemisphere in a strange search for something he did not know, for something which probably was an ultimate or entity. His was a way of life, of waiting composed, of a continual search. It might have been a face for which he looked or a certain evening in time. Yet it seemed always that it must be every face, every evening, for he went on and could not ignore his restlessness and dissatisfaction.

"I believe, primarily, he was an idealist, one such as few men are. He knew that a man stagnates in security; he knew that mutation was the only permanence, that the fragile crystal of idealism must be maintained by self or else suffer decimation. So he was simultaneously, a realist of the strongest mold who was estranged from mundane realism by an incomprehensive breech.

"He had a great love for people yet it was not indiscriminate for hate was parallel. Perhaps his greatest fault was that he loved too universally, that his sensitivity was so varied, rather than restricted as is the sensitivity of others, and so complicated as concerned reactions that it was too large an endowment for a single man. Loneliness breeds well in such a disposition and it seemed at times that he was possessed of the loneliness of all men. There were times that he cursed what he said were his in-bred philosophies, for he could not admit division of self; he could not reconcile diversification. He was too conscious of distinct personality to make himself one in the experiment of man-woman relationships. Even the great jaw of isolation was insufficient to allow him to condone what to him had become a cultural or social definition of male-to-female harmony. Resentment grew within him. He pondered the instituted demands, those elements of human nature which founded nations and held that love was of permanence. As was all great beauty to him, so was love – ephemeral, lost to writhing fogs of the invariable.

"He could find no woman who could recognize frailty, be magnanimous before inevitability. He desired love. Yet he could not accept that which had been cast about it, that which had been bred into people, which was to his mind a bleak inheritance. So he was without that thing which was vital within him, which rose as chilled air in his chest before tormented being. Perhaps it was as Santayana, I believe, said; *Understanding too much to be ever imprisoned, loving too much to be ever in love.*

"But he was human and an ageless rhythm would make him one of the generations of the world. He would take a woman, cruelly, for she was a spirit in his loneliness, and for a few brief moments, love with the love of all the ages. Then he would leave, as he must, and the love untarnished, a moment singular and undiminished by inconstancy, by the shadow which would have made of it hate."

Hart sipped his port for a moment. "That is the story of a man I know yet whom, basically, I don't know. A man bound within himself by desires too vigorous to be satiated, by obscurities which completed the motivations of his living. Your man, Berntzen, knew his life. This man of whom I speak remained a stranger to himself, always in a pursuit, always pursued; always a search, one who waits."

Hart set his glass down. There was silence about the table.

"A strange story," Berntzen said. "A man thinks of himself. I could not be such a man."

"Metaphysics – most deny it. Shadows are not admitted. Nor should I like to be as that chap was," Jonathan Wright said.

The captain pushed his chair back and stood. Everyone stood. Hart went out on the promenade deck and gazed out at the sea. Marcia Wright joined him and leaned on the rail before him. The sea was calm. There was no breeze – only a dead, insufferably warm, motionless air.

"It was you in that story."

64

"Yes."

"Then you'll be leaving me, too." Her voice was hardly audible, her hand trembled on his arm.

"It has always been so; a strange proportion of desire and helplessness."

Marcia closed her eyes for a moment before saying, "I'll follow you. I can't let you leave. I'll not surrender you to an enigma. I won't ..."

"No, you won't follow me." He gestured to the ominous blackness of the sky behind the ship. Great masses of cloud billowed and twisted, whirled and writhed as though stirred by a giant hand.

Marcia looked in silence. A tremor passed over her body. The insane forces evident in the tormented mists seemed to press against her throat, to stifle any sound she might wish to make. She turned weakly to Hart and hid her face against his shirt. "No, it will be no enigma this time," he said. His face twitched slightly but his voice was calm.

A thin, high-pitched hum sounded through the air overhead, torn currents whispering in terrible mockery of the madness to be unleashed upon them. Hart leaned against the rail of the ship, with one arm about the girl, and waited.

They tell now a story on the shore of Sumatra of the steamer MANFREN out of Liverpool, which was crushed against the Soenda Strait, and of the bearded old man who lives in the hut on the beach near the scene of the wreck. He merely waits and his face twitches. They say he's quite mad.